P9-CRZ-247

UNDERGROUND CHRISTMAS

BY JON HASSLER

Staggerford
Simon's Night
The Love Hunter
A Green Journey
Grand Opening
North of Hope
Dear James
Rookery Blues
The Dean's List

FOR YOUNG READERS

Four Miles to Pinecone
Jemmy

FORTHCOMING

Days Like Smoke: Recollections of a Happy Boyhood

UNDERGROUND CHRISTMAS

JON HASSLER

Afton Historical Society Press
Afton, Minnesota

© 1999 by John Hassler
All rights reserved
First edition

No part of this book may be reproduced or transmitted in any form
or by any means, electronic or mechanical, including photocopying,
recording, or by any information storage and retrieval system,
without permission in writing from the publisher.

Library of Congress Cataloging-in-Publication Data

Hassler, Jon.
     Underground Christmas / Jon Hassler. -- 1st ed.
          p.   cm.
     ISBN 1-890434-09-4
     I. Title.
PS3558.A726U53   1998
813 .54--dc21

Printed in Canada.

The Afton Historical Society Press is a non-profit organization
that takes pride and pleasure in publishing fine books.

W. Duncan MacMillan   Patricia Condon Johnston
president   publisher

Afton Historical Society Press
P.O. Box 100
Afton, MN 55001
800-436-8443

For my son David

UNDERGROUND CHRISTMAS

1

WE'RE A PARTY OF FOUR MEN sitting in the abbey root cellar, which, since my day as a student on this campus, has been converted into a potting shed. The gardener, our host, has served us several beers and is passing around a box of very good cigars when Novice Nick blurts out his confession that a certain campus secretary—a blond bombshell he calls her—is testing his vocation.

"The registrar sent the two of us down to the

room where they keep old records, and she brushed against me like she was looking for it. I mean, my God, what's a guy supposed to do?"

Charlie thinks this is funny. Charlie's a seminarian, and about twenty years younger than the rest of us. Sitting high on the potting table, he grins down at me and says, "You know her, don't you, Jay—the blonde that's givin' Nick fits? Her name's Millie, in the registrar's office."

"No, I guess I don't."

"Sure you do. The one with the build, and all that hair piled on top of her head."

My mind's eye quickly takes in the registrar's office, but to no avail. Which is no surprise. Since my arrival here last summer I've been so busy licking my wounds that I've been scarcely aware of my surroundings.

Comes the oracular voice of the gardener from behind his cloud of smoke: "Just remember, Nick, avoid the occasion of sin and you'll be all right."

"Avoid it? How do I avoid it? She comes right up to me and . . ."

"Easiest thing in the world. Don't leave the office with her."

"But the registrar sent us down there together, to bring back two boxes of records."

Charlie pipes up again. "Registrar must be pullin' your leg, Nick—records are all on computer these days."

"Not all of them," says Nick, sounding a little peeved at Charlie's facetiousness. "Not the old ones. That's what I'm there for, to get the old records on-line. We've got records going back to the nine-teenth century."

Nick is fairly old for a novice—my age if not older, and I'm fifty. He's a balding little man with a crooked spine who's spent most of his adult life working at a Potlatch paper plant way up near the Canadian border. I don't know if he's ever been married. Now approaching the end of his novitiate year, he will soon have to decide whether to commit himself to the monastic way of life or go back to his job as bookkeeper/timekeeper/computer-expert at Potlatch.

I can tell this is a serious problem for Nick by the way he reduces his speech to a mumble each time he speaks of the woman, and the way he won't look us in the eye. He's sitting on a low stool and speaks with his eyes on the doodles he's drawing in the dirt floor with an old, bent trowel he's picked out of the gardener's tool box. He's having trouble keeping his cigar lit.

The gardener, who goes by the name of Brother Godwin, leans forward out of his cloud to relight Nick's cigar with the stub of a church candle, and he asks him, "Now tell me, have you and her done anything . . . you know . . . yet?"

The novice doesn't have to reply. His reddening face is his answer. Charlie's laugh is interrupted by a smoky cough, then he laughs some more.

Brother Godwin, sinking back into his chair, advises, "You better ask Father Abbot to change your work assignment."

Nick, scratching away at the hard-packed dirt, nods his head, but says nothing.

"See Father Abbot," Brother Godwin repeats. "That's the beauty of joining the community, you're never alone with your problems. The abbot's always there with his fatherly advice. And remember this, Nicholas, the untested vocation isn't worth very much."

Brother Godwin, needless to say, is not one of the great minds of Benedictinism. Look around and you see that when Vatican Two swept over the world, it missed this fellow's garden shed. Tacked to the four-by-four pillars holding up the roof are little crosses cut from the fronds of Palm Sunday; beside the doorway stands a plaster incarnation of Our Lady; and hanging over the work table, between a pipe wrench and a tattered old clipping from *Newsweek* concerning the Pope's visit to Iowa, is a phosphorescent purple crucifix. And just as his sacramentals have not been altered in his twenty-five years as a monk, neither have his perceptions of himself and God and everyone else in between. He takes pleasure in dispensing Ultimate Answers, as though drawn from a child's catechism. Got a personal problem? "See the abbot." Novice Nick's Potlatch stock? "A monk has no use for money." My son Bob in drug treatment (yes, our talk has covered Bob as well)? "If he's only twenty, he's young enough to be cured." The quality of popcorn? "The abbey always buys Jolly Time."

I remember Brother Godwin from my student days. He was a novice himself back then, hoeing the vast vegetable garden the monks used to maintain and which was abandoned when the college outgrew the abbey's ability to be self-sufficient. Food now comes in by truck. Hardly a day passes that I don't see a grocery jobber carrying his order book into the food service area beneath my second-floor office in Bede Hall.

"You hear me?" Brother Godwin insists. "See the abbot—tell him your story."

Novice Nick snaps, "Father Abbot's already changed my job twice. He's liable to throw me out on my ear."

"So what's the difference? He throws you out or you leave with the bombshell?"

Nick chuckles bitterly. "Hell of a difference." He risks a glance in my direction. "Only a monk'd have to ask what the difference is, am I right, Jay?"

I tip my head in a neutral sort of nod, while restraining myself from speaking up. I want to say, For God's sake Nick, don't be timid, either forget her or run away with her—make up your mind! But I keep my mouth shut. It's not my place to tell other people how to live their lives. Besides, I don't want Brother Godwin preaching platitudes at me. It's just that I can't stand ambiguity these days. I want everybody to be predictable. It's crazy, I know. It's a product of my divorce and my son's attempted suicide. I mean, I've always been inclined toward the status quo, but I never used to be neurotic about it.

Charlie jumps off the potting table and puts another stick of wood in the stove—damp wood judging by the sizzle. "You know it's cold in here Brother Godwin?" He points to my feet. "Your guest of honor is sittin' here in his li'l ol' oxfords freezin' his toes off. You gotta get yourself a fan to circulate this heat."

Despite our age difference, Charlie is the closest

thing to a friend I've got on this campus. He's one of the smiliest guys you'll ever meet. His smile is constant, like an idiot's. At first I thought he might actually be an idiot, but no, his mind has a very nice edge to it, and it used to bother me that he was wasting it on the study of theology. Medieval Studies or Canon Law okay, but Metaphysics, Moral Theology, Epistomology? —come on, why would anyone want to get into all that useless speculation? I was about to put this very question to him one day when he said something that shut me up before I got a word out. "You know, Jay," he said, "in my four years in this seminary I have read exactly one hundred books I didn't understand." Wow! No worries here, I thought. With candor like that, Charlie's going to make one hell of a priest.

I'm not a seminarian, but I live in the seminary because that's where the empty rooms are these days. Last spring, divorcing my wife and desperate to leave the college in Rookery where she and I had offices side by side in the Literature and Languages Division, I accepted this one-year professorship at my alma mater. The day I arrived on this campus in the woods, Charlie was the first person I met. He helped me carry in my belongings—two suitcases, a coffeemaker, and a lawn chair—and he laughed and laughed when I told him this was all I was left with after the divorce settlement. My wife got the house, the cabin, the newer car, and the dog.

"Actually this belongs to her too," I said, holding up the flimsy lawn chair, "but she kindly let me take it." Charlie couldn't stand up he laughed so hard. He collapsed on the sunny grass and shook with laughter. From that moment on, I loved the guy. I'd tried everything to get over my anger, my despondency; I raged, I wept, I prayed, I tried Prozac—I'd done everything but laugh. But I wasn't laughing yet on the day I moved in. I went on to describe for Charlie the courtroom scene last June, and how Judge Lawton Anderson—said to be one of the fairest judges in Minnesota—awarded Susie everything but the coffeemaker (Susie doesn't drink coffee), the clothes in my closet, and the old Toyota with its broken hatchdoor, its wobbly steering, and its 160,000 miles. And all the while her boyfriend Scuyler was sitting at the back of the courtroom gloating over what he assumed would belong to him and her together, the poor sap. Charlie laughed so hard I thought he was going to hyperventilate.

"Hell," I raged, "by the time I left town she'd ditched him for another lover whose name is Sarah."

Charlie was so weak with laughter I had to help him back to his room.

He's going to be ordained in the spring. I won't see much of him in the meantime; the day after New Year's he'll begin his four-month internship as deacon at the Cathedral parish in Berrington. It was by Charlie's invitation that I am attending this little gathering in the potting shed. Although the seminary and monastery stand at opposite ends of the campus, Charlie in his four and a half years here has become well acquainted with the monks, particularly with the manual laborers in the woodworking shop, the print shop, the gardens, the woods, and the roadways. He was reared on a farm himself, in southern Illinois, which accounts for his aw-shucks drawl.

Despite the chuffing of the stove, the dirt floor of this cellar is very drafty; the snow we brought in on our shoes still lies in chunks by the door. "Thanks for the beer and cigar," I tell Brother Godwin around ten thirty when my feet turn numb.

"Why so early?" he wants to know. "We usually try and catch an hour or so of David Letterman." He opens the cupboard next to the potting table and reveals a TV, CD player, and radio.

"Not tonight, I've got to drive to Rookery tomorrow. I like to visit Bob every other weekend."

"Well, come again," he says. "Take Charlie's place. It's going to be lonesome around here next semester."

"Thanks, I'll be glad to drop in, but not as Charlie. I don't have his good humor."

"Good," says Novice Nick with conviction, apparently having seen enough of him.

As we trudge up the snowy hill to our rooms, Charlie asks me if I enjoyed myself.

"Sure," I tell him. "Next time I'll wear over-shoes."

"Knew you'd like ol' Godwin, he's a good ol' boy."

"I never smoked a better cigar."

"Oh, the cigar was special. Usually it's some smelly old stogie. He keeps back the good ones for special occasions."

I'm flattered to think that an English prof's appearance in the potting shed should be special. I want to hear Charlie say so; therefore I ask, "What's special about tonight?"

This stops him in his tracks. He grabs my sleeve and finds my eyes in the moonlight, stares into them and speaks very slowly: "You really don't know, do you."

I forgot. It's Christmas Eve.

2

CHRISTMAS MORNING DAWNS FROSTY and
eighteen below—much too cold, I decide, for
trekking across campus to attend Mass and risking
another illness. Shortly after moving in last August,
between summer session and fall semester, I came
down with a cold that blossomed into the four-
day flu, and believe me, it's no fun lying sick in an
empty building the size of St. Andrew's Seminary.
For hours at a time the only sound to enter my

ears—every thirty-four seconds—was the automatic flushing of the urinals down the hall.

And I have a second, even better, reason for skipping Mass. While the few seminarians remaining here over the holidays are occupied with their liturgy, I will have the breakfast room to myself—which shows you the sorry state of my religious devotion these days. I assume it's temporary. I figure my spiritual impulses will return to me as soon as Bob gets out of treatment and I get used to being divorced. You see, last spring when Susie told me she was moving over to the Randolphs' house so that she and Sarah Randolph could explore their relationship, my world turned upside down. I was actually speechless. I remember not saying a word until I got Sarah's husband on the phone and instead of the commiseration I expected, he said, "Pray about it, Jay, that's what I'm doing." Well, I blew my stack. I mean, I laid into Jerry Randolph, of all people, a man who's been doing everything right all his life, a real pillar of the community—trustee of the hospital, little league coach, bingo caller for the Knights of Columbus—an all-around sweet, innocent guy, and here I am calling him a bunch of awful names. I don't remember what names, but there were a lot of them. All I remember is my charming manner of signing off. I shouted, "Go to hell, you sleazy pimp," and I slammed down the phone, and that's the last thing I ever said to my friend Jerry Randolph.

I wrote him a letter from St. Andrew's, told him I didn't have my head on straight, told him how sorry I was for saying outrageous things. I didn't tell him what set me off in the first place: his telling me to pray about it. He never responded.

The seminary breakfast room is in the basement. I don't remember ever being so fond of basements as I've been since I moved here. In a basement, you feel so secure, and here especially, where you have not only this womblike protection from the hurtful things of the world, you have beauty as well: walnut paneling, indirect lighting, white tablecloths on sturdy oak tables. Plus, with your housemates still at Mass, you have the luxury of silence besides. What better place, in other words, to clear your head of ugly dreams and wake up with coffee and the morning paper? This morning, however, instead of the newspaper, I am browsing through Merton's *Seven Storey Mountain*, looking for a piece of wisdom I seem to recall from my student days when this book was a standard text in freshman religion class. I'm scarcely into chapter one when—bad luck—I hear someone coming down the stairs, no doubt Sammy DeSmet, who likes to skip out of Mass early.

"Jay, have you got yourself a hangover?" It's not Sammy, it's Charlie, dragging himself over to the shelf of cereal boxes. " 'Cause I feel like the last rose o' summer the cat dragged in, Jay. What was Brother Godwin givin' us last night? Hey, you don't look sick even a tiny little bit."

I close the book. "Moderation in all things, Charlie."

"Much obliged for your wisdom." He sits across the table from me, looking very pale, pours milk over his corn flakes, and digs in. With his mouth full he asks, "What you readin'?"

"Thomas Merton."

"Merton." He nods, chewing. "We studied him in undergrad. English poet of the eighteenth century."

"No, no. Twentieth-century American monk."

"You mean he didn't write 'Elegy in a Country Churchyard?'"

"Time was when you couldn't even set foot on this campus without knowing your Merton."

He takes a swig of orange juice, wipes his mouth and says, "Jay, I'm leaving."

"I know, for Berrington."

"No, I mean for good."

I spill my coffee.

"Yep, I'm checkin' out. Gonna get me a job in Chicago. Been on my mind lately how academic I've

got, how far off I am from the workaday world. I've
let myself get soft. How can I minister to people as
a priest o' God without gettin' my hands dirty in the
workaday world?"

"Charlie, you can't quit now." I swallow twice,
trying to wring the anguish out of my voice. "In six
months you'll be ordained."

"Don't feel much like bein' ordained this year—
maybe another year. What I feel like is goin' out and
gettin' my hands dirty, out in the workaday world."

"Charlie, you are out of your mind!"

He smiles. "How can I counsel people if I don't
know the first thing about real life on the outside?
Jay, do you realize I been in boarding schools since
the ninth grade? Why, I'm so well grounded in
philosophy that for my leisure readin' I pick up

Wittgenstein or Nietzsche instead of the Sunday funnies. I'm a weirdo, is what I am Jay, just a downright, eggheaded weirdo."

I keep a lid on my anger. "Charlie, don't do something you'll be sorry for."

"What do I know about drivin' the freeway? Why, do you realize I haven't driven a car since two years ago last summer? What do I know about makin' money? I'm gonna start the new year by findin' myself a job."

"Doing what?" I demand.

"Don't know. My education sure is a worthless commodity on the outside. As a layman I could do parish work, but that doesn't pay diddly. I need to make lots of money."

"You do?"

" 'Course I do. If I don't go out there with the idea of bein' successful, in the way the world understands success, then I'm not gonna learn much, am I? I don't intend to stand off to the side of life. I intend to be in the mainstream."

I'm losing my best friend just as I lost my wife, and I'm devastated. The difference is that this time I'm not speechless. I begin with my voice lowered. "I've heard this all before, Jay. It's a widespread belief these days that in order to minister to people you have to adopt their ways. It sounds perfectly logical, but I've never believed it. I call it the quicksand principle. I've never believed you can pull somebody out of the quicksand by jumping in yourself."

"Jay, I need to be in the mainstream," he

repeats, as though he hasn't heard a word I uttered. "What do I know about having to go shoppin' in those awful shoppin' centers in the evening after puttin' in a full day's work at a job I hate? What do I know . . ."

"Listen to me, you dope. You don't need to know that stuff. If you leave now, you'll never come back, I'm certain of that. You'll never be a priest. You're a little too earnest when you talk about money, your eyes glow with desire when you mention the shopping centers you pretend to despise."

My rising voice causes him to look wary. "Jay, take it easy, I'm prepared to make mistakes."

"But you're not prepared to correct them. I see it now, plain as day. Within a year you'll be married, and how do you correct that?"

"Who'd want to?"

"Don't interrupt me! And before you know it, you'll have four kids and a string of carwashes from Chicago to Evanston called Charlie's Wash and Wax. You'll be famous for your placards nailed to the walls with quotations from Nietzsche and Wittgenstein. You'll be the carwash king of northern Illinois and parts of Wisconsin."

Charlie laughs. Instead of making him see the light, I'm making him laugh, which makes me boil over. I pound the table, shouting, "I see a gigantic billboard as you go north out of the city. It's your goddam carwash billboard and it shows Big Bird saying, 'I wash, therefore I am.'"

I get up to leave the room, leave him sitting there, his elbows on the table, his face buried in his handkerchief, his shoulders shaking with silent laughter. But no, he isn't laughing. As I step away from the table, he removes his handkerchief and looks after me with tears in his eyes.

I feel terrible. Climbing the stairs, I'm already planning my apology. I had no business lecturing him on what course his life should take. What's come over me? I never used to be so meddlesome, so selfish. I've got to stop flying off the handle, or I'm liable to wind up in the state hospital with my son Bob.

And Thomas Merton agrees with me. In my room, I open the book to this: "Without silence our language is meaningless—the silence between word and word, between utterance and utterance."

3

ROOKERY LIES FOUR HOURS NORTH of
St. Andrew's, between Paul Bunyan State Forest and
oblivion. Traffic is light, virtually all holiday visitors
having already got where they're going. Stopping for
coffee and gas in Brainerd, I notice that the few of us
left on the road are mostly men like myself, traveling
alone, with colorfully-wrapped presents on the back
seat and the gray look of fatigue and anxiety in our
eyes. Divorced or estranged fathers, we're spending

Christmas Day on the road in hopes that a beloved child somewhere will love us in return.

I can't say for certain whether Bob loves me. He's always been hard to read. During his boyhood, I always thought of his reticence as part of his charm. He had an engaging little smile for polite occasions and a restrained little chuckle that told you he was greatly enjoying himself. During his teens this quality used to drive his mother nuts. "Bobby, will you please show some emotion!" she would call to him, during one of his track meets, say, or at the graduation party we threw for him. She'd long ago given up saying it to me.

Likewise, Bob had the stoic's way with pain and disappointment. I learned too late that his frown meant he was severely troubled, that his barely audible groan pointed to disaster. It was last spring that he came in from college near midnight and shook me awake, saying, "I'm expected to know all my lines by Friday, Dad. I can't possibly learn them all by Friday—there are over a hundred." He was a freshman, planning to major in Dramatic Arts. I turned over in bed and looked at him, and because I saw no real distress in his expression, only a slight scowl, I didn't realize he was out of his mind. He then said, "I need a break, Dad, let's go to Switzerland for the weekend. I'll take my script along. Or Norway. I could really concentrate in Norway."

Assuming he was kidding, I told him to get some sleep, and the instant he understood I wasn't taking him seriously he gripped my arm so tightly he left bruise marks. "Please, Dad, come with me," he

pleaded. "Get dressed and come with me to Norway
. . . just for a coupla days . . ."

I don't know what he'd been indulging in that
evening. I assumed it was some kind of upper given
to him by a friend—a one-time mistake. What I did-
n't know, and what came out in treatment, was that
he'd been secretly drinking vodka and using crack for
the better part of a year. Already at nineteen our Bob
was—without our catching on—a hopeless alcoholic
and drug addict.

I say hopeless because he literally lost all hope.
He hit bottom the day I packed up my belongings to
move to St. Andrew's. I was carrying out my last box
of books when I saw him standing in the street
beside his little Honda CRX. He looked as if he was
about to drive off somewhere. I went over to him

and said good-bye. His response was a mumble—I expected no more—and then he surprised me with the tightest embrace of my life. He must have held me for fifteen or twenty seconds, and all the while he was making this strange sobbing or groaning noise in my ear. Then he hopped into his car and drove away. I noticed that he didn't buckle himself in—because, as he later told me, he stood a better chance of dying that way.

It was only about eight blocks and two stop-lights from our house to the city limits, and yet by the time he hit the open road he was up to eighty-five miles an hour with a patrol car chasing him. He wasn't a mile from town when he turned off the highway and smashed into a power pole—not by accident, he later admitted. Because the pole was standing in a deep ditch, the car tipped sideways as it left the roadway and Bob was thrown flat across the front seat an instant before the pole tore the top off the car at windshield level. Bob came out of it with a concussion, a traffic citation, and a judge's order that he enter treatment. Had he worn his seat belt, he'd have been decapitated.

He went into treatment a zombie. Whether from trauma or drugs, he spent a week sitting deep in a couch with his eyes open and seeing nothing. I delayed my move to St. Andrew's and went to the hospital every day. I talked to him, trying to bring him back from wherever his mind had taken him. I talked until my voice wore out, mostly about some great games of pool we'd played together, but to no avail. After a while he'd turn and look at me as if to say, Who the hell are you?

We used to play a lot of pool, Bob and I. Some families, I'm told, relate to one another around the dinner table. Others go camping in the woods. Some fathers take their sons fishing. From the time Bob was in junior high, the pool table had been our meeting ground. At least once a week for years we went downtown to Oren's Beer Joint, where the green table felt is worn and torn, and there we'd play what we called Bob and Jay's World Series of Pool. The loser of four games out of seven not only paid, but was expected to blame his loss on the poor condition of the tables and the crooked cue sticks. Whenever I lost, which came to be well over half the time, Bob would give me a fatherly pat on the back and say, "Sorry, old man, better luck next time." Come spring it will be two years since we played a game of pool.

He was in treatment seven days before he came out of his trance—and just in time, since his counselors were about to kick him out (the goons!) for being uncooperative. His expression didn't change—he was still somber—but at least he was aware of his surroundings. I can't tell you how relieved I was. I remember saying, later, to Charlie, "Now I know how Lazarus's sisters felt when they saw him step out of the tomb."

But he's not the same son I used to have. He can't seem to warm up to me. He'll come around, his counselor tells me, recovery is slow. I've returned to Rookery twice a month to visit him, and each time, driving into town, I've prayed to God—as I'm praying now—that the two of us might recover something of our lives as father and son. To be met with a little embrace would be enough, not necessarily the bear hug he gave me the day he tried to take his own life. Or even a pat on the back would do it. Even a touch.

At the edge of town I stop along Fast-Food Avenue and come away with Christmas dinner. It's nearly two o'clock when I park in front of Bungalow Eight. I switch off the ignition and sit there a moment, rubbing my eyes, and suddenly my passenger door opens and Bob gets in and falls upon the sacks of food. So much for the embrace I'd hoped for.

While I eat a fish sandwich, he eats a Big Beef, a double cheeseburger, and a bag of fries. He's looking very healthy these days, heavier, more robust, happier than he's looked in years. Between bites he answers my questions about treatment. His only complaint is about the few men who don't cooperate with the counselors. "We vote on whether to keep 'em in or kick 'em out, and we always vote to keep 'em in. I think we ought to kick 'em out." A year ago, having said this, he would have shut communication down until tomorrow, having used up his daily limit of words. Now he goes on about his counselor, his daily schedule, his fellow residents. Can this articulate young man be my son?

He says he'll complete the twelve-step program in late January, but then—a great surprise—he wants to stay on and enroll in the counseling program. He admires his bungalow's counselor—Andy is his name—and he'd like to emulate him.

"What? You've given up your dream of being an

over-the-road truck driver?"

"I have." He turns to me with an indulgent little smile. "That was junior high, Dad."

"And how about your dream of being a
roustabout?"

He shakes his head, staring out at the jack-
pines and scrub oaks. This remark doesn't deserve a
denial. His desire to leave town with the circus last
year was no doubt drug-induced.

"How about acting? You're giving up theatre?"

"Maybe I can do that on the side. You know,
community theatre, that kind of thing? I just figure,
as a counselor . . ." He gives me a shy glance. "I
could do more good for humanity." Then he adds,
"Like you and Mom have been doing all your lives."

He holds me in his gaze while it dawns on me

that this is the most—the only—heartwarming statement I've heard in months. I want to tell him so. "Bob," I begin, but he opens his door and gets out before I can finish.

He takes me for a sightseeing walk across the grounds, showing me what he's accomplished as a member of the hospital's groundskeeping crew. "We hung all these big electric candles up on these lampposts." "See that fence over there—we just put that up last week." "Did you notice the road is smoother? We've been patching it with hot tar."

At the top of a windy hill I point out that I'm not dressed for the wintry outdoors. "Sorry," he says, and we hurry off toward Bungalow Eight. On the way he asks me, "How am I doing, Dad? How do you think I'm doing?"

"Wonderfully, Bob. You're doing wonderfully."

"All along here, come spring, we're going to have flower beds. We're going in with a roto-tiller and plow up this whole area and plant geraniums and a bunch of other stuff. It'll be the first thing you see when you drive in."

He is doing wonderfully. You'd never know he's living in a treatment center. His eyes are clear. So is his talk. He's shaven and neatly dressed. And yet he isn't my son. My son has never spoken at length on any subject. He might be some anonymous groundskeeper running on about his work, and I his anonymous visitor.

Bungalow Eight has been Bob's sprawling, pine-paneled home since August. He points out the circle of chairs in the front parlor, left over from this morning's group sessions.

"Even on Christmas?" I ask.

" 'Specially on Christmas. There's certain guys get all screwed up thinking about Christmas. Come on back to my room."

His room, judging by the number of beds, is actually a ward shared by five men. On one of the beds lies a sleeping Indian. He's wearing a tight blue shirt, his jet-black hair is long and lustrous, and he's sleeping with his mouth open. A neatly groomed middle-aged man sits at a table chewing on a pencil and writing, probably, a letter. An older man, with a bushy white mustache, has followed us into the room. Bob introduces us for the sixth or eighth time. This is Andy. He gives me a brief nod and then begins lecturing Bob on how to handle tomorrow's examination, an oral interview on the subject of Bob himself, the answers to which will determine if he is to be considered a candidate for counselor training. Standing by a window and paging idly through a magazine, I listen to their jargon. "What's coming down?" "I'm all right with that." "I know where you're coming from." Like grammarians, computer hackers, and literary critics, those in treatment have evidently developed an insiders' language all their own. Finishing his instructions, he nods again in my direction and hurries away, telling Bob he has faith in him. "Cool," says Bob.

We return to the parlor, where we buy two Cokes and sit at the window watching the people come and go in the parking lot. The majority of residents are accompanied by two generations of visitors (spouses and parents), and some by four (youngsters and grandparents as well). Here and there I spot a parent listening intently to something a son or daughter is saying. Oh, the fortitude required in pretending to be interested in such drivel. I spent the past several months listening patiently to Bob come up through the phases of recovery, the blaming phase, the guilty phase, the parroting-his-counselor phase.

A man goes by with his arm around a boy, and I wonder if it's this that sets Bob off. "Dad," he says, studying his Coke can, "I have to tell you, you don't look so hot."

"Aw, go on." I get halfway to my feet and smile into the mirror behind Bob. What's the problem? I might look a little tired, a little clenched, but I see nothing worse than weariness in my expression.

"No, really, Dad, you're not yourself. Probably nobody's told you, but you go around with this scowl on your face all the time, like you're mad at the world."

"I ain't mad at nobody," I tell him, quoting an old blues ballad. I'm about to explain that what he takes to be anger is fatigue, but he doesn't give me a chance.

"Well, whatever it is, it's very off-putting," he tells me. "It's a look I remember from when I was little and you were getting your doctor's degree. I wasn't allowed in your study till you were done, remember? Well, who'd want to go in there anyway, I used to think. I'd peek in and you'd have a book open and you'd be scowling at it.

"Bob, do you know what I was doing? I was

writing the most boring dissertation ever conceived in the witless mind of any graduate committee anywhere on the face of this planet: "Moral Choice in the Novels of Enid Bagdanovitch." Read five pages of Ms. Bagdanovitch, Bob, and you'll see why I was scowling. She's the wordiest, most depressing, godawful . . ."

"Okay, so it's not anger, it's depression, which is really suppressed anger. Did you know that, Dad? Andy says depression is really suppressed anger. I'm not blaming you in any way, Dad. You've been through hell. I mean, Mom moves out and then your only kid tries to kill himself. I'm only pointing out that for the last six, eight months you haven't been the same dad I used to know. It's like you're—I don't know—so distant all the time. I had to bring it up, Dad. One thing I've learned in this room is that straight talk is better than clamming up and never saying stuff."

Another one of his roommates enters the bungalow, a sallow-faced young man named Dan, along with his mother and father. Bob introduces us and we stand there making small talk, but I'm not paying attention. My mind is on Bob's straight talk. Of course he's right. My doctoral work was very depressing. They were anxiety-filled years of make-work research with nothing at the end but the degree itself. Nothing learned except how to scowl. And now for the past several months, instead of Enid Bagdano-vitch, I've been studying myself and not caring much for what I see. I see a man consumed by fear.

Dan and his parents proceed down the hallway and Bob sits down again. I stand at the window and ask, "You know what I'm feeling, Bob? I'm feeling

. . ." It behooves me to explain myself, and yet

"fear" is such an embarrassing little word to utter

in connection with oneself. I need to tell him, since

he brought it up, that ever since my life fell apart last

summer I've been waiting for the next thing to go

wrong. I've been walking tentatively, afraid that a

misstep will cause the rest of the floor to give way. I

need to tell him about my phobia concerning change.

My fear of change has grown so out-of-hand, in fact,

that I feel a surge of resentment every time a food

truck arrives on St. Andrew's campus, where there

used to be vegetable gardens, a kitchen full of bakers,

livestock grazing in pastures. I can't stand to see

people change the course of their lives. I need to tell

him about Charlie, and how, in my obsession for the

status quo, I blew my top and left the poor man in tears on Christmas morning. I need to tell him about Novice Nick and how he was spared a similar outburst only because I was afraid of what Brother Godwin would say. I need to tell him what happened to my old friendship with Jerry Randolph. I need to spill out my soul to my son.

And maybe I will, next trip. But for now I'm speechless, for Bob has his arms around me, and I'm fighting back tears and shuddering. When I gain control of myself, I turn away and try to say "Thanks," but it comes out like a quack. I blow my nose and am about to try it again when Bob pats me on the shoulder and says, "Sorry old man, how about a game of pool?"

"Pool?" My voice has a tremor in it. "I didn't

know you had a pool table."

"Sure, down here." He opens a door off the parlor and flicks a light switch, revealing a flight of descending stairs. He starts down, saying, "Come on, the cues are straight and the table's fairly new, so you'll have to think up another excuse."

I follow my son the counselor into the basement.

———

ABOUT THE AUTHOR

Jon Hassler, Regents' Professor Emeritus at St. John's University in Minnesota, has published 11 novels. His first, STAGGERFORD, was chosen Novel of the Year (1977) by the Friends of American Writers, and GRAND OPENING was chosen Best Fiction of 1987 by the Society of Midland Authors. A screen version of A GREEN JOURNEY was produced in 1990 as an NBC Movie of the Week, starring Angela Lansbury and Denholm Elliot. All of Jon Hassler's novels, including his latest, THE DEAN'S LIST, are available as Ballantine paperbacks. In 1996 he was granted an Honorary Doctor of Letters degree by the University of Notre Dame.

Recently retired after 42 years as an English teacher in various Minnesota high schools and colleges, Jon Hassler lives with his wife Gretchen in Minneapolis, where he is at work on his memoirs.

Designed by
Barbara J. Arney
Stillwater, MN

Typeface is
Trump Mediaevel

Cover Illustration by
Charles J. Johnston
Afton, MN